# The Secret Garden

Illustrated by Alan Marks

Retold by Susanna Davidson

Based on a story by Frances Hodgson Burnett

The last time Mary Lennox saw her parents
was in the garden outside their house, in India.

That night, a terrible fever swept through the house.
Mary's mother and father both died.

Mary felt as if she were all
alone in the world.

Then a letter arrived from her
uncle, Mr. Craven,
inviting her to England to stay.

Misselthwaite Manor,
Yorkshire, England

Dear Mary,

I have made arrangements for you to come
to England and live at Misselthwaite Manor.
My housekeeper will meet you in London
and escort you here.

I'm afraid I won't see you for some time as
I have to travel to Europe on business.

Yours sincerely,

Archibald Craven

"I don't like it here," thought Mary,
as she crossed the wild, windswept moors.

She arrived at the house late at night.

Her uncle was away, the housekeeper said,
and left her alone in a shadowy room.

Outside, the wind howled like a lonely person.

In the morning, Mary wandered out of the house into a wintry garden, where an old man was digging.

"What's behind that wall?" she asked.

"Ah," said the gardener.
"That's the secret garden. Mr. Craven shut it up when his wife died. Then he buried the key and went away."

As he spoke, a robin fluttered up and perched nearby.

He cocked his head and looked at Mary.
"Will you be friends with me?" she whispered.

"You sound just like our Dickon," said the gardener.

"He talks to all wild things.
Now run along, missy. I've got work to do."

Mary watched the robin fly off and decided to follow him.
"Show me the key to the garden," she begged.

The robin swooped down, and hopped around on the ground.

"He *is* trying to show me something,"
thought Mary.

She scrabbled in the soil
and found... a rusty key.

Mary searched and
searched for the
door to the
garden.

Then, one day, when the wind came
in sweet-scented gusts from the moor, she found it.

She put the key in the lock
and the door creaked slowly open...

Mary was inside
the secret garden.

It was a magical, mysterious place.

A hazy tangle of rose branches and
spiky green shoots thrust up
through the wintry ground.

Mary spent all morning in the garden, entranced.

The shoots looked so crowded, she cleared spaces around them.

The robin chirped, as though pleased someone
was gardening here at last.

Outside, she saw a boy with a fawn by his side.

"Are you Dickon?" she asked shyly.
He nodded.

"Can you keep a secret?"
Mary asked.

"I keep secrets all the time," Dickon replied. "Secrets about
fox cubs and birds' nests. Aye, I can keep a secret."

"Come with me," whispered Mary,
and led him to the secret garden.
Dickon looked around as if in a dream.

"I never thought I'd see this place," he murmured.
"Help me make it come alive," said Mary.

"Yes," whispered Dickon.
"We'll make it the prettiest garden in England."

The winter passed into spring.
One blustery night, Mary couldn't
sleep. She was woken by a cry
that pierced the wind.

She followed it
down dark passages,
until she reached a door
with a glimmer of light beneath.

Inside the room was a vast carved bed
with a boy in the middle of it, sobbing.

"Are you a ghost?" whispered Mary.

"No!" he snapped. "I'm Colin Craven."

"Mr. Craven's my uncle," said Mary.
"Are we cousins? Why did no one tell me about you?"

"I'm not well," Colin replied. "My mother died when
I was born and my father can't bear to look at me."

"Just like the secret garden," said Mary.

And she told him all about it...
the sun and rain and buds bursting into flower,

while Colin closed his eyes
and dreamed of a garden, coming alive.

Mary raced to Colin's room
the next morning.

"I've brought a friend
to meet you," she said.

"Will you take me to the garden?" asked Colin.

They rushed down the
paths. Mary flung back
the ivy and opened the
garden door.

Sunshine lit up sprays of flowers
and the air was alive with birdsong.

"I can feel things growing," gasped Colin.

"You can work with us in the garden," said Mary.

Colin's pale face grew rosy in the sunlight.
"And maybe I'll get well," he whispered.

Every day they played and worked in the garden
and, every day, Colin grew stronger.

"If only my father could see me," thought Colin.

And he began to wish,
"Come home, come home."

One night, Colin's father, far away in Italy,
had a strange dream. He heard his dead wife calling his name.

"Where are you?" he pleaded.

"In the garden,"
came the reply.

Mr. Craven returned home at once. He rushed to the garden.

As he came down the path,
    he heard children laughing behind the wall.

"How can that be?" he thought.
"The garden must be dead...
I buried the key."

At that moment, Colin and Mary burst out of the garden door.

"Colin?" gasped his father. "Is that really you?"

"I'm better, Father. I'm well at last.
It was Mary, and the garden."

"The garden..." he murmured, "just like my dream."

"It's a magical garden," said Mary.
"Come inside and see."

Taken from an adaptation by
Mary Sebag-Montefiore

Edited by Jenny Tyler & Lesley Sims

Designed by
Louise Flutter

This edition first published in 2012 by Usborne Publishing Ltd, 83-85 Saffron Hill, London EC1N 8RT, England.
www.usborne.com Copyright © 2012, 2008 Usborne Publishing Ltd. The name Usborne and the devices ♈ ⊕ are Trade Marks
of Usborne Publishing Ltd. All rights reserved. No part of this publication may be reproduced, stored in a retrieval system,
or transmitted in any form or by any means, electronic, mechanical, photocopying, recording or otherwise,
without the prior permission of the publisher. First published in America in 2012. UE.